KEEP A POCKET IN YOUR POEM

KEEP A POCKET IN YOUR POEM

CLASSIC POEMS
and
PLAYFUL PARODIES

Written and Selected by J. Patrick Lewis

Illustrated by Johanna Wright

WORDSONG

AN IMPRINT OF HIGHLIGHTS
HONESDALE, PENNSYLVANIA

INTRODUCTION

SOMETIMES, WHEN I READ A WONDERFUL POEM, I want to write a parody of it. For me, this is the best way to pay tribute to someone else's work.

Of the hundreds of poems I admire, here are thirteen that appealed to the tinkering part of my brain. (Of course I could have tinkered with many others.) So I took the poems apart and put them back together, but in my own words.

What is a parody (or "parroty," as I like to call it, after the bird that is our greatest mimic)? A poem is a parody if it imitates another poem in style and subject matter. The poems I parody in *Keep a Pocket in Your Poem* are happy, sad, light, dark, humorous, or serious.

My intention was not to try to write *better* poems than the originals. All credit goes to the wordsmiths who inspired me. But what fun— and what a challenge it is!—to take a well-known poem and echo it by tweaking and twisting to make it new.

Why not try writing a parody yourself? Pick one of your favorite poems and write a poem like it. You might just find, in the beginning, that this is a terrific way to jumpstart your writing; and in the end, you'll have a poem that will honor the original poet.

—JPL

TABLE OF CONTENTS

Keep a Poem in Your Pocket

Beatrice Schenk de Regniers

Keep a poem in your pocket
and a picture in your head
and you'll never feel lonely
at night when you're in bed.

The little poem will sing to you
the little picture bring to you
a dozen dreams to dance to you
at night when you're in bed.

So—
Keep a picture in your pocket
and a poem in your head
and you'll never feel lonely
at night when you're in bed.

Keep a Pocket in Your Poem

J. Patrick Lewis

Keep a pocket in your poem
filled with every wondrous thing
you can think of—red hawk feather,
silver penny, pinkie ring,

Yo-yo, M&M's, a ticket
from a roller coaster ride,
pictures of your pug—a poem
needs a pocket on the side.

So—
Keep a pocket in your poem,
for imagination grows
from the deepest secret pockets
every pocket poet knows.

Stopping by Woods on a Snowy Evening

Robert Frost

Whose woods these are I think I know.
His house is in the village, though;
He will not see me stopping here
To watch his woods fill up with snow.

My little horse must think it queer
To stop without a farmhouse near
Between the woods and frozen lake
The darkest evening of the year.

He gives his harness bells a shake
To ask if there is some mistake.
The only other sound's the sweep
Of easy wind and downy flake.

The woods are lovely, dark, and deep,
But I have promises to keep,
And miles to go before I sleep,
And miles to go before I sleep.

Stopping by Fridge on a Hungry Evening

J. Patrick Lewis

Whose mold this is I think I know.
My mother won't admit it, though;
She hates it when I peek inside
To watch her fiendish fungus grow.

My little sister cried and cried
To see a pound cake . . . *petrified!*
That quart of milk's about to *blast.*
The cottage cheese has multiplied!

The mustard's green, the mayo's past
The expiration date—not *last*
November?! No, it can't be true.
The algae's brown and creeping fast.

The eggs are black, the meat is blue!
There's only one thing left to do:
Get the hose and hire a crew,
Get the hose and hire a crew.

Winter Sweetness

Langston Hughes

This little house is sugar.
   Its roof with snow is piled,
And from its tiny window
   Peeps a maple-sugar child.

Winter Warmth

J. Patrick Lewis

This little book is cocoa.
   It warms me when it steams,
And from its toasty pages
   Spiral my marshmallow dreams.

from The Goblin

Jack Prelutsky

There's a goblin as green
As a goblin can be
Who is sitting outside
And is waiting for me.
When he knocked on my door
And said softly, "Come play!"
I answered, "No thank you,
Now please, go away!"

The Ogre

J. Patrick Lewis

There's an ogre as wide
As a flatbed truck
On my porch. He's got teeth
Like a gator's—all buck.
When he roars, "What's for lunch?!"
Something buckles—*my knees!*
But he grins when I cry,
"Macaroni and cheese?"

15

Mice

Rose Fyleman

I think mice
Are rather nice.

Their tails are long,
Their faces small,
They haven't any
Chins at all.
Their ears are pink,
Their teeth are white,
They run about
The house at night.
They nibble things
They shouldn't touch
And no one seems
To like them much.

But *I* think mice
Are nice.

Rats

J. Patrick Lewis

I think rats
Are really brats.

    Their teeth are sharp,
    Their hearts are black
    As charcoal from
    The love they lack.
    They're rightly known
    As evildoers
    Who hatch their wicked
    Plots in sewers.
    Some folks who fail
    To see the threat
    May keep one as
    A household pet.

But *I* think rats
Are brats.

Cocoon

David McCord

The little caterpillar creeps
Awhile before in silk it sleeps.
It sleeps awhile before it flies,
And flies awhile before it dies,
And that's the end of three good tries.

Armadillo

J. Patrick Lewis

The little armadillo steps
Across the yellow line, and schleps
Itself—a needlepoint woodchuck—
In front of an enormous truck . . .
Then waddles home. (Beginner's luck!)

19

from "Hope" is the thing with feathers

Emily Dickinson

"Hope" is the thing with feathers—
That perches in the soul—
And sings the tune without the words—
And never stops—at all—

Grief is the thing with tissues

J. Patrick Lewis

Grief is the thing with tissues
For mopping up the tears,
So when you are in bed at night,
They won't fill up your ears.

The Eagle

Alfred, Lord Tennyson

He clasps the crag with crooked hands;
Close to the sun in lonely lands,
Ring'd with the azure world, he stands.

The wrinkled sea beneath him crawls;
He watches from his mountain walls,
And like a thunderbolt he falls.

The Firefly

J. Patrick Lewis

She climbs late summer skies and sends
Important messages to friends . . .
Confetti blinkers on rear ends.

Who knows which meadow she came from
Through cricket and cicada hum?
But look, she's waltzed onto my thumb.

Infant Innocence

A. E. Housman

The Grizzly Bear is huge and wild;
He has devoured the infant child.
The infant child is not aware
He has been eaten by the bear.

Grizzly Bear Reality

J. Patrick Lewis

The pinkish Infant Child turns red,
Especially when she's not been fed.
The Grizzly Bear was unaware
A hungry child could eat a bear.

Fog

Carl Sandburg

The fog comes
on little cat feet.

It sits looking
over harbor and city
on silent haunches
and then moves on.

Hail

J. Patrick Lewis

The hail flies
on furious hooves.

It batters cars
and rooftops,
slamming anger,
and then melts away.

This Is My Rock

David McCord

This is my rock,
And here I run
To steal the secret of the sun;

This is my rock,
And here come I
Before the night has swept the sky;

This is my rock,
This is the place
I meet the evening face to face.

This Is My Tree

J. Patrick Lewis

This is my tree,
And here I climb
To grasp the endlessness of Time.

This is my tree,
And here I trace
Its limbs against the reach of Space.

This is my tree,
And from this berth
I take the measure of the Earth.

Happy Thought

Robert Louis Stevenson

The world is so full of a number of things,
I'm sure we should all be as happy as kings.

Sleepy Thought

J. Patrick Lewis

The world is so full of a number of dreams,
I'm sure all our pillows should burst at the seams.

FOR PAULA,
OUR MOTHER'S MINISTERING ANGEL

—JPL

FOR BILLY

—JW

ACKNOWLEDGMENTS

"Keep a Poem in Your Pocket" from *Something Special* by Beatrice Schenk de Regniers. Copyright © 1958, 1986 by Beatrice Schenk de Regniers. All rights renewed and reserved. Used by permission of Marian Reiner.

"Stopping by Woods on a Snowy Evening" from *The Poetry of Robert Frost*, edited by Edward Connery Lathem. Copyright © 1923, 1969 by Henry Holt and Company, copyright © 1951 by Robert Frost. Reprinted by permission of Henry Holt and Company LLC. All rights reserved.

"Winter Sweetness," 1994 by The Estate of Langston Hughes; from *The Collected Poems of Langston Hughes* by Langston Hughes, edited by Arnold Rampersad with David Roessel, Associate Editor. Used by permission of Alfred A. Knopf, an imprint of the Knopf Doubleday Publishing Group, a division of Penguin Random House LLC. All rights reserved.

"The Goblin" text copyright © 1977 by Jack Prelutsky. Used by permission of HarperCollins Publishers.

"Mice" from *Fifty-One New Nursery Rhymes* by Rose Fyleman, text copyright © 1931, 1932 by Penguin Random House LLC. Copyright renewed 1959 by Rose Fyleman. Used by permission of Delacorte Press, an imprint of Random House Children's Books, a division of Penguin Random House LLC. All rights reserved.

"Cocoon" and "This Is My Rock" from *One at a Time* by David McCord. Copyright 1952 and renewed © 1980 by David McCord. Used by permission of Little, Brown Books for Young Readers.

"Fog" from *The Complete Poems of Carl Sandburg*, Revised and Expanded Edition. Copyright © 1969, 1970 by Lilian Steichen Sandburg, Trustee. Reprinted by permission of Houghton Mifflin Harcourt Publishing Company. All rights reserved.

Text copyright © 2017 by J. Patrick Lewis
Illustrations copyright © 2017 by Johanna Wright

All rights reserved.

For information about permission to reproduce selections from this book, contact permissions@highlights.com.

WORD∫ONG
An Imprint of Highlights

815 Church Street
Honesdale, Pennsylvania 18431
Printed in China

ISBN: 978-1-59078-921-6
Library of Congress Control Number:
2016942423

Production by Sue Cole

First edition

The text of this book is set in Freight and Boho Serif.
The drawings are done in acrylic paint and ink on canvas, then are scanned and digitally fine-tuned.

10 9 8 7 6 5 4 3 2 1